Bubble Gum
Rescue

READ ALL THE CANDY FAIRIES BOOKS!

Candy Fairies

Bubble Gum Rescue

HELEN PERELMAN

ILLUSTRATED BY
ERICA-JANE WATERS

ALADDIN
NEW YORK   LONDON   TORONTO   SYDNEY   NEW DELHI

ALADDIN

An imprint of Simon & Schuster Children's Publishing Division

1230 Avenue of the Americas, New York, NY 10020

First Aladdin paperback edition July 2012

Text copyright © 2012 by Helen Perelman

Illustrations copyright © 2012 by Erica-Jane Waters

All rights reserved, including the right of reproduction in whole or in part in any form.

ALADDIN is a trademark of Simon & Schuster, Inc., and related logo is a registered trademark of Simon & Schuster, Inc.

For information about special discounts for bulk purchases, please contact Simon & Schuster Special Sales at 1-866-506-1949 or business@simonandschuster.com.

The Simon & Schuster Speakers Bureau can bring authors to your live event.

For more information or to book an event, contact the Simon & Schuster Speakers Bureau at 1-866-248-3049 or visit our website at www.simonspeakers.com.

Designed by Karina Granda

The text of this book was set in Berthold Baskerville Book.

Manufactured in the United States of America 0719 OFF

6 8 10 9 7 5

Library of Congress Control Number 2011934219

ISBN 978-1-4424-2217-9

ISBN 978-1-4424-2218-6 (eBook)

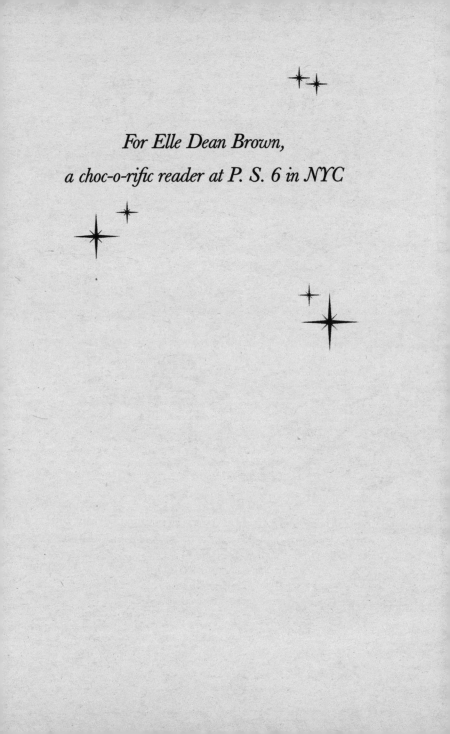

For Elle Dean Brown,
a choc-o-rific reader at P. S. 6 in NYC

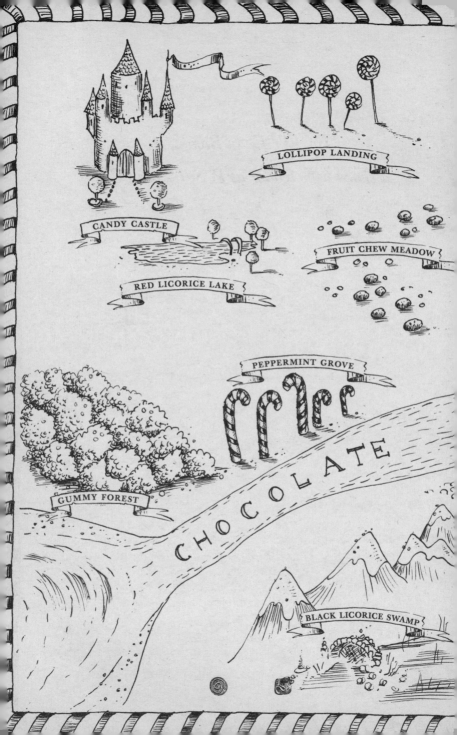

CHOCOLATE WOODS

CARAMEL HILLS

CHOCOLATE FALLS

CANDY CORN FIELDS

SOUR ORCHARD

THE FROSTED MOUNTAINS

R I V E R

MARSHMALLOW MARSH

CANDY
Kingdom

SUGAR
VALLEY

Contents

CHAPTER
1

A Sticky Mess

Early in the morning, Melli the Caramel Fairy flew to the top of Caramel Hills. She was checking on the caramel chocolate rolls she had made with her Chocolate Fairy friend Cocoa. Melli smiled at their newest creation drying in the cool shade of a caramel tree. Yesterday the two fairies had worked hard rolling small logs of caramel and then dipping them in chocolate. The final touch was a drizzle of butterscotch on top. Melli couldn't wait to taste one!

A caramel turtle jutted his head out of his shell and smelled the fresh candy. Melli laughed. "You were hiding over by that log," she said to the turtle. She kneeled down next to him. "Did you think you'd snatch a candy without my noticing?"

The turtle quickly slipped his head back into his shell. Still as a rock, he waited to see what the Caramel Fairy would do.

Melli placed one of the candies in front of him. "Of course you may have one," she said sweetly. "There's enough to share."

The turtle stuck his head out again and gobbled it up.

"Do you like the candy?" Melli asked.

The turtle nodded, and Melli smiled. "Cocoa and I are going to bring these to Sun Dip this evening," she said.

Sun Dip was the time at the end of the day when the sun set behind the Frosted Mountains and the Candy Fairies relaxed. Melli loved visiting with her friends and catching up on everyone's activities. And today she and Cocoa would bring their new candy. She hoped her friends would enjoy the sweet treat.

Just as Melli was putting the candies in her basket, she heard a squeal. It sounded like an animal in trouble. She put the basket down and walked toward the sound.

"Hot caramel!" Melli cried as she peered around one of the caramel trees.

 3

Lying on the ground was a small caramella bird. He was trying to flap his wings to fly, but they were barely moving. Melli leaned in closer and noticed that the bird's feathers were wet and stuck together.

Melli reached out to the bird. "You poor thing," she whispered. She tried to calm the little one by talking to him. Caramella birds lived in the valley of Caramel Hills and had bright yellow wing feathers. They lived off the seeds of the caramel trees and filled the hills with their soft chirps.

"Where have you been playing?" Melli asked sweetly. She carefully picked up the bird and gently stroked his head. Immediately she realized that his feathers were covered in thick butterscotch. "How did you get coated in this syrup?" she asked. "No wonder you can't move or fly."

The bird chirped loudly. It was shaking in her hands.

"Butterscotch is not the best thing for feathers," Melli said, smiling at the tiny caramella. "Don't worry, sweetie," she added softly. "Let's give you a good bath and get this mess off your wings. I know all about sticky caramel." She patted the bird's head gently. "I will get you cleaned up in no time. Let's go to the water well and rinse you off."

Melli held on to the bird and flew to the edge of Caramel Hills. The tiny creature seemed to relax in Melli's hands, but his heart was still pounding. At the well Melli began to wash the butterscotch off the bird's wings. She knew she'd have to spend some time scrubbing. She

 5

had gotten caramel on her clothes before, and it often took a while to get all the goo off.

After a few rinses Melli began to see his brightly colored feathers.

"There, that does it," she said, feeling satisfied. She stood back and looked at the little bird. "You do have gorgeous yellow wings!"

The bird shook the water off his wings. He was happy to be able to move them freely. He bowed his head to Melli, thanking her for helping him.

"You should be able to fly now," Melli said. "Be careful, and stay away from the sticky stuff!"

"Hi, Melli!" Cocoa appeared next to her. "What are you doing here?"

"Cocoa," Melli gasped. "You scared me! I didn't see you there." She pointed to the caramella bird.

"Look who I found. He was covered in butter-scotch, and his wings were stuck together. I just gave him a bath with the fresh well water."

Cocoa's wings fluttered. "Oh, bittersweet chocolate," she said sadly. "This is worse than I thought."

"What are you talking about?" Melli asked. "He's all clean now. He'll be able to fly."

"It's not only this bird I am worried about," Cocoa said. "I heard from a sugar fly that there was a butterscotch syrup spill on the eastern side of Butterscotch Volcano. That must be where this one got syrup on his wings. *All* the cara-mella birds are in danger!"

"Oh no," Melli said. "So many caramella birds live over there. What else did the sugar fly tell you?"

"That was all," Cocoa replied.

Sugar flies passed information around Sugar Valley. If a fairy wanted to get the word out about something important, the sugar flies were the ones to spread the news.

"Let's go now," Melli said urgently. "If Butterscotch Volcano erupts, there'll be a large spill in the hills." She looked down at the bird. "Is that what happened to you? Will you take us to where you got butterscotch on your wings?"

The bird took flight, and Melli and Cocoa trailed after him. His yellow feathers gleamed in the sunlight. Melli beat her wings faster. She was very concerned about what kind of sticky mess they were going to find.

CHAPTER 2

Butterscotch Volcano

Melli grabbed Cocoa's hand. She couldn't believe the sight below her. Butterscotch Volcano was in the middle of Caramel Hills, and a place where Caramel Fairies often gathered. Once a year at the Butterscotch Festival, a few brave and experienced Caramel Fairies would dip into the volcano for a supply of hot butterscotch.

The extra-sweet syrup was then stored in large barrels in Candy Castle and used throughout the year for special candy projects.

Melli's eyes widened as she saw the thick syrup pooled in the large area east of the volcano. The land was flat, and the caramella birds built their nests there. Now it was a lake of syrupy butterscotch. Melli shook her head in disbelief. Never before had she seen butterscotch ooze out of the volcano. While there was hot butterscotch syrup deep within the volcano, there had not been an eruption in a long, long time.

As Melli flew over the volcano with Cocoa she squeezed her friend's hand tighter. "No wonder that little bird got his feathers sticky," Melli said. She pointed down below—butterscotch was *everywhere*!

"The sugar flies were definitely right about this," Cocoa said. "This is a supersticky mess."

"Did you send the sugar fly to Raina, Berry, and Dash?" Melli asked. If things were this bad, she wanted all her friends to know. Together, the five of them could work to help the caramella birds of Caramel Hills.

Cocoa nodded. "Yes, I sent them each a message," she replied. "I hope they can get here fast."

Melli carefully observed the area. "Look, Cocoa, the butterscotch isn't coming from the *top* of the volcano," she said. She pointed to the top, which was clean and dry. "Where do you think it's coming from?"

Cocoa squinted and then flapped her golden wings. "Let's get a better look," she said bravely.

The two friends flew down closer to the volcano. The sight broke Melli's heart.

"The poor birds," Melli said softly. "This is their home, and now it's a sticky, syrupy mess. "

"They can't even move," Cocoa added. She saw many birds trying to flap their butterscotch-coated wings.

As Melli looked around she suddenly spotted her sister, Cara, perched on a caramel tree. "There's Cara," she said. "Maybe she knows what's going on."

Cara was rubbing a small bird's feathers with a sponge. She was dipping the sponge in a pail of water when Melli and Cocoa landed next to her.

"Oh, Melli!" Cara exclaimed. "I'm so happy you came! We need all the help we can get. This spill is spreading fast."

"How did this happen?" Melli asked. She knelt down next to her sister.

"The volcano cracked, and there's a leak on its side," Cara explained. "I heard the older Caramel Fairies talking."

"Bittersweet," Cocoa muttered.

"All this butterscotch is oozing out of the volcano?" Melli gasped. She shook her head. "This is gooier than I thought!" She held out a little caramel for the bird Cara was cleaning. "Sweet thing," she cooed.

Cara rinsed the bird's feathers again. "This one is going to be okay," she said. "But there are so many others. I'm not sure we'll be able to wash them all."

"That's why *we're* here to help!" Berry said, landing next to Cara.

"We got the sugar fly message," Dash told Melli.

"And we came as fast as we could," Raina added.

Melli was touched that all her friends had gotten to Caramel Hills so quickly. She smiled at the Fruit Fairy, Mint Fairy, and Gummy Fairy standing before her.

The fairies immediately started to care for the butterscotch-coated birds. As they worked Melli kept looking around. The flow of syrup was steady, and the spill was growing larger.

"Raina, why do you think this happened?" Melli asked.

Raina usually had the answers to questions.

She loved to read and was known to have memorized many sections of the Fairy Code Book. The thick volume of the history of Sugar Valley had helped the friends solve mysteries around Candy Kingdom in the past.

"Butterscotch Volcano is dormant," Raina said. "That means it doesn't erupt for long periods of time." She paused and glanced at her friends. "This doesn't mean that it *couldn't* erupt."

"And we know there is butterscotch in there because the fairies filled barrels at the Butterscotch Festival," Dash added.

"Dash is right," Melli agreed. "But it took a week to fill all the barrels at the castle." She glanced over at the volcano. "No, this is very different. I want to go take a closer look. Anyone want to come?"

"I will," Cocoa called. "I've never seen so much butterscotch syrup!"

"We're *all* going with you," Berry said.

Raina and Dash lined up next to the Fruit Fairy. They had finished cleaning a bird and were worried about the amount of syrup too.

All five fairies flew up in the air. Melli took a fast dive near the volcano. Her friends followed.

"Look!" Melli shouted. "There's the crack on the side of the volcano! The older Caramel Fairies were right. It's enormous!"

"No wonder there is an overrun of syrup," Cocoa said.

"A leaky volcano?" Dash asked, wrinkling her nose.

They all looked to Raina. She shrugged. "It can happen," she said. She peered down at the

 17

volcano. "Maybe there was an eruption that made the volcano crack?" She tapped her finger to her chin. "That seems the most likely answer."

"Hot caramel," Melli muttered.

"You mean hot butterscotch," Dash said, correcting her.

"This isn't good news at all," Cocoa said.

"No, it's not," Melli replied. She looked at her friends. "The question is, how do we stop this butterscotch burst?"

CHAPTER 3

Big Burst

The fairies huddled together on a branch of a caramel tree. From where they were sitting, they could see the butterscotch spreading.

"We have to do something—and fast," Melli said.

"Those poor birds," Raina whispered as she looked below. "The butterscotch in their wings

will keep them from flying. They'll never be able to get food."

Melli felt helpless. Usually she adored Butterscotch Volcano and the rich syrup that was inside. Making candies with the fresh, hot butterscotch was always a highlight of the Butterscotch Festival. Melli loved watching the brave Caramel Fairies dip into the center of the volcano to scoop out the sweet, golden treat. She had never imagined how dangerous the volcano could be!

"The butterscotch is out of control," she said sadly.

Dash flew off the branch and quickly circled the area. When she came back to the branch, she had a sour look on her face. "If we don't stop the leak, the butterscotch will reach Chocolate

Woods. Think of all the animals there—and the chocolate crops!"

"Double-dip bittersweet," Cocoa said, hanging her head.

"We need to stop this," Berry said, sitting down next to Melli.

"Maybe we should be asking *whom* to stop?" Melli asked.

"Mogu?" Cocoa asked. She wrinkled her nose. "Do you think that salty old troll could have done this?"

Melli shivered. The thought of Mogu in Caramel Hills upset her. The greedy troll often tried to steal Candy Fairy candy, but he usually stayed under his bridge in Black Licorice Swamp. She looked to her friends.

"I'm not sure if this is his style," Berry said,

thinking aloud. "The butterscotch from the volcano is yummy, but it's not in candy form. You'd have to do a lot of work to make candy, or have the patience to wait for the butterscotch to cool."

"Doing work and having patience don't seem like Mogu's style," Raina said, agreeing with Berry.

Cocoa fluttered her wings and looked around. "But if Mogu is greedy enough, he might."

"No, Mogu wouldn't be patient enough," Melli said with certainty. "Having patience is one of the hardest parts of being a Caramel Fairy."

"Which is why I like to work with mint," Dash said, grinning. She reached into her pocket and took out a peppermint. "Ahh," she said. "Quick and tasty!"

 24

Melli smiled at her minty friend. No one liked speed better than her friend Dash. She was one of the smallest Candy Fairies, and also one of the fastest. *And* the least patient fairy she knew!

"The more I think about it, I think it's possible the crack just happened naturally," Raina suggested. She slipped the Fairy Code Book out of her bag. "Yes, I have the book," she said to her friends before they could comment. Usually one of her friends couldn't help making fun of her for always having the fact book on hand. In the past the thick volume of the history of Sugar Valley had helped the friends solve mysteries that happened in Candy Kingdom.

"Let's hope there's something in the book that can help us figure out this sticky mess," Melli said.

As the fairies hovered over the book Melli heard her sister call to her.

"Let me go check on Cara," she said to her friends. "I'll be right back."

Down at the bottom of the tree, birds surrounded Cara.

"Melli," Cara gasped when she saw her big sister. "There are so many sticky caramellas! Two Caramel Fairies just left more here for us to clean." Cara's brown eyes were full of tears. "How will we ever save them all?"

Melli hugged her sister. Seeing her so upset made Melli stronger. "We will help one bird at a time," she said. "If we work together, we can figure this out." She pointed up at the tree behind them. "Raina is looking up some facts in the Fairy Code Book. She's sure to find some useful information."

"I hope so," Cara said. "In the meantime, this area will be the rescue center. I'm going to get some more supplies. Can you stay here? I think more caramellas will be coming."

"Sure as sugar, I'll stay," Melli said. She watched her sister fly off, and then she picked up a sticky bird. She carefully wiped its wings and tried to get the syrup off.

Suddenly the sounds of gurgling and rumbling filled the air. It sounded as if a giant was awaking from his slumber. Melli froze. She looked toward the volcano. The crack she had spotted earlier was now split open wider. More butterscotch rolled up to Melli's feet. The spill was getting deeper and deeper . . . and more dangerous for everyone in Caramel Hills.

Cara came up behind her. "Oh no," she

moaned. "More butterscotch! What are we going to do?"

"I'm going to see if the other fairies have come up with a plan," Melli said. "Will you be all right?"

"Yes," Cara said bravely. "I'll work on cleaning the birds. You work on stopping this spill!"

Melli smiled at her little sister. "I'm so proud of you," she said. "I'll try to be back soon."

Soon, she thought, *before this mess gets bigger.*

4

Chocolate Aid

Melli rushed back to the caramel tree where her friends huddled together. Raina was in the middle of the group with the Fairy Code Book on her lap. Melli hoped that while she had been with Cara the fairies had thought of a plan. This latest burst of butterscotch from the volcano had created even more trouble.

"We're in a hot butterscotch emergency," Melli cried as she flew up to the tree. "Now the spill is even deeper than before!"

"Take a breath," Cocoa told Melli. "We can't panic. We need to focus." She held out her hand to Melli. "Come sit down for a minute." She moved over to make room on the branch for her friend.

Melli knew Cocoa was right, but seeing more butterscotch flow from the volcano was upsetting. "It's getting worse down there," she said sadly.

"More butterscotch?" Dash asked. Her blue eyes were wide and full of fear.

"But we found something in the Fairy Code Book that might work," Raina said, giving Dash a stern look. "Remember, we have to remain calm." She held up the book to show Melli the picture. "We could build a barricade to block the butterscotch from spilling out into Chocolate Woods," Raina said slowly. "The idea is from this story about an overflow from Chocolate River."

"A barricade?" Melli said as she studied the picture.

"You see, Chocolate Fairies used bark and branches from a chocolate oak tree and tied them together, " Cocoa explained. "The bundle blocked the flow of chocolate coming from the rising river."

"The barricade saved Chocolate Woods," Berry added.

Melli bit her nails and looked up at her friends. "But butterscotch is much thicker and stickier than chocolate from Chocolate River. Will a chocolate barricade really work?"

Cocoa put her arm around Melli. "Chocolate Woods is so close. Let's get some chocolate branches and bark and give it a try."

"Chocolate is not the strongest material. It tends to flake," Dash pointed out.

Cocoa scowled at Dash. "We should at least try."

Melli turned to Dash. Everyone was feeling the pressure of the situation, and Melli didn't want her friends to fight. But Dash was a master at building sleds. She was one of the fastest racers in Sugar Valley and had even made her own sled and won a medal at the Marshmallow Run sled race. "Dash, do you have another suggestion?" Melli asked.

Dash looked down at the ground. "I don't know what would hold the syrup back," she said quietly. "Especially hot butterscotch."

The friends all glanced down at the spill.

"Cocoa is right," Melli said, breaking the silence. "Chocolate Woods is nearby and the easiest place for us to get materials. At least we can try to keep the spill from spreading so fast."

The fairies nodded in agreement. They flew off to the woods and gathered pieces of bark, twigs, and branches from the chocolate oaks. They put the materials on a large blanket, and each fairy took a corner. Melli flew in front to lead the way.

For the first time since she had seen the spill, Melli had a feeling of hope. Now if only this chocolate barricade would solve the problem!

 34

Near the base of the volcano the five friends put the chocolate logs and bark on the ground. When the last of the wood was unloaded, Melli stood back and held her breath.

"Look!" she cried out. "The barricade is working!"

Butterscotch wasn't passing through the chocolate barricade. The five fairies joined hands and did a little dance. But their rejoicing didn't last long. After a few moments their feet were covered in the thick golden syrup.

Cocoa hung her head. "You were right, Dash," she said. "I'm sorry."

"We had to try," Dash said. "I'm really sorry that this didn't work. The chocolate wasn't strong or sticky enough to hold back the butterscotch."

Melli's wings fluttered and a smile appeared on her face. "Dash! That's it!" she exclaimed. Her feet lifted off the ground as she fluttered her wings. "That's the answer!" she shouted. Her friends stared at her, amazed at her outburst. "We need something that will be sticky and sturdy for sealing the crack," she said.

Raina, Cocoa, Dash, and Berry waited for Melli to explain.

"Bubble gum!" Melli finally exclaimed. She saw that her friends still didn't understand her idea. "If we can get enough sticky bubble gum, first we'll seal this crack, and then we'll be able to plug it up and stop the butterscotch from leaking!"

Raina considered Melli's plan. "I think you're on to something. Bubble gum would be an excellent choice. It's strong and sticky, and it would fill up the crack. But we'll need a lot of it."

"My cousin Pinkie makes bubble gum," Melli said enthusiastically. "She can help! She works at Candy Castle."

"Well then, let's go see her now!" Berry said.

Melli quickly wrote a sugar fly message to Cara explaining that she would be back shortly—

with another plan. Melli hoped this time their idea would work. Already there were too many birds harmed by the butterscotch spill.

"Let's hope this is a pink solution that will stick!" Melli said as she took the lead and flew toward Candy Castle.

CHAPTER 5

Think Big

When the five fairies arrived at Candy Castle, there was a large group of fairies gathered in the Royal Gardens. The guards had just sounded their caramel horns, and Princess Lolli was standing on her balcony. The kind and gentle ruler was trying to quiet the crowd just as the fairies landed in the garden.

"Look!" Melli said. "We're just in time for Princess Lolli's announcement."

"Unfortunately, we've seen firsthand what is going on in Caramel Hills," Raina said. "I'm sure that is what she is going to talk about."

"Shh," Berry scolded. "She's ready to speak."

"Good afternoon," Princess Lolli said to the fairies in the Royal Gardens. "I know many of you have heard about the trouble in Caramel Hills. It is a very sad day." The princess looked around at the crowd. "There is a large crack near the base of the volcano, and hot butterscotch is leaking out into the hills."

Heavy sighs were heard throughout the crowd.

If only they could all see what is happening there now, Melli thought sadly.

"The caramella birds that live up in the hills are in the greatest danger," Princess Lolli continued. "We need to work together to stop the spill and clean the animals that have been covered in the hot butterscotch."

"The news certainly has traveled fast," Cocoa said, looking around the Royal Gardens.

"We'll need everyone's help in the kingdom," Melli said. "I'm so glad to see so many fairies here."

"Sugar Valley is under a Kingdom Emergency," Princess Lolli declared. "All fairies are expected to help out in Caramel Hills. I hope to have more news for you soon." The princess turned to her right and waved her hand. Tula, one of Princess Lolli's advisers, appeared. "Tula will head the cleanup project. Please see her so we can get started as soon as possible."

The princess bowed her head and stepped back into the castle. Everyone felt her sadness. Princess Lolli was a good friend to all the creatures in Sugar Valley. Melli knew that this news was weighing heavily on her heart.

"Come," Melli said to her friends. "Let's go talk to Princess Lolli. I want to tell her about my plan."

The fairies flew into the castle. They waited patiently while the palace guard asked permission for them to enter the throne room. They found Princess Lolli near the window, looking out toward Caramel Hills.

"Princess Lolli, Caramel Hills is so awful," Melli blurted out. She ran up to the princess. "The caramella birds are trapped in the thick, hot butterscotch."

Princess Lolli gave Melli a tight hug. "I know," she said. "This is very disturbing news."

"But, Princess Lolli, we have a plan," Melli said, brightening. "A plan we think will work."

"At first we thought that if we could barricade the butterscotch, we could stop the leak, but that didn't work," Cocoa confessed. "The chocolate wood wasn't strong enough to hold the hot syrup."

"So instead, we thought we could seal the crack," Melli added.

Princess Lolli turned to face the five fairies before her. Her eyebrows shot up. "Tell me more," she said.

"My cousin Pinkie makes bubble gum here at the castle," Melli said. "If we can help her make enough sticky bubble gum, we might be able to mend the side of the volcano."

44

Princess Lolli smiled. "That is a fantastic idea," she said. "I am so impressed, and I'm grateful for your creative thinking." She walked over to her throne and sat down. "I think that is certainly worth a try!"

Melli was ready to burst with pride.

"Have you spoken to Pinkie?" Princess Lolli asked.

Melli shook her head. "We wanted to see what you thought about the idea first," she said.

Princess Lolli looked back out the window toward Caramel Hills. "Let's hope Pinkie can make enough gum."

"We'll help her," Melli offered.

"Thank you," Princess Lolli said. She called for one of the guards. "Please find Pinkie and ask her to come to the throne room at once." Then she faced Melli. "I must go speak to Tula before she leaves for Caramel Hills. You and your friends wait here for Pinkie. I'll be back shortly."

Melli and her friends looked at one another in amazement. They had been in Princess Lolli's throne room before, but they had never been there alone. They stood very still, not sure what to do.

Suddenly Melli began pacing around the room. "I hope Pinkie gets here soon."

"She'll be here," Cocoa told her. "Don't worry."

A short while later Pinkie flew into the throne room. She hugged Melli and her friends. She had heard about the Butterscotch Volcano disaster but had not realized how serious it had become. When Melli filled her in, her eyes started to brim with tears.

"And so we need to stop the leak in the

volcano," Melli said. "We thought your bubble gum could be the plug."

Pinkie tilted her head and flapped her pale pink wings. "I'm not sure I can do that," she said.

This was not the reply Melli had expected to hear. Her wings drooped down to the floor.

"I only make tiny pieces of bubble gum, Melli," Pinkie said. She dipped her hand into her pocket and pulled out three minia-ture gumballs.

Melli glanced up at her friends. Then her eyes settled on Princess Lolli's throne. The tall, wide peppermint sticks that Dash had created for the princess made the throne extra-special.

Melli thought back to when Dash had been growing the peppermint sticks for the princess's new throne and training for the Marshmallow Run. No one had believed that Dash could both manage her training and create the large royal peppermints, but she had. Melli moved closer to Dash.

"When you were making the peppermint sticks for the throne, they were the biggest sticks you had ever made, right?" Melli asked.

Dash nodded. She reached into her bag for a snack.

"Did you do anything differently?" Melli asked.

Taking a nibble of her treat, Dash shook her head. "Not really," she said.

"They took longer to grow, but those sticks are the same as the small ones right here." Dash showed off a smaller peppermint stick in her hand.

"And I bet those taste the same," Cocoa said, smiling. She winked at Melli. She knew exactly what her clever friend was doing.

"Sure as sugar!" Dash exclaimed.

"You see, Pinkie," Melli said, jumping up, "it's still the same bubble gum. You just have to make much, much, much more."

"We can help you create the most bubble gum ever," Raina said. "You can do this, Pinkie!"

"We're all counting on you," Melli told her.

Pinkie looked concerned, but Melli hoped Dash's peppermint sticks would inspire her cousin—and change her mind.

A Sugar-tastic Idea

Melli's wings twitched as she waited to hear Pinkie's reply. She hoped her cousin would agree to make a superbig bubble gum plug for the volcano. Waiting for her to answer was so hard! She crossed her fingers. Then she listened to her four friends, who surrounded Pinkie.

"We're asking for your help for all the cara-mella birds in Caramel Hills," Cocoa said.

Melli shot her friend Cocoa a grateful look.

"Maybe if you went to Caramel Hills and saw the problem close-up, you'd understand why we desperately need your help," Raina said. "You could see what your bubble gum will do."

Melli was thankful for Raina's calm and thoughtful response. And it seemed to help Pinkie with her decision.

The small Bubble Gum Fairy fluttered her wings. She raised her eyebrows and let out a deep breath. "Will you all come with me?" she asked.

"Sure as sugar!" the five friends said in unison.

The fairies flew out of Candy Castle and

 51

across the kingdom to Caramel Hills. As they flew along Chocolate River, Melli glanced over at Pinkie.

"I know this seems crazy to you," Melli said. "But I really think bubble gum is the answer."

Pinkie nodded. "I need to see the problem before I try to make a solution," she said.

Melli understood. She hoped that when Pinkie saw the cracked volcano, she'd realize why bubble gum was their best shot at fixing the leak. She led Pinkie and her friends straight to Butterscotch Volcano. At the bottom of the volcano Melli spotted Cara and flew down to greet her.

"I'm so glad you're back," Cara blurted out. "The butterscotch is spreading fast—and heading dangerously close to Chocolate Woods."

"It would be a disastrous and delicious mess in Chocolate Woods," Dash said with a wistful look in her eyes.

Melli knew that Dash often thought with her stomach first. She smiled at her, knowing that she meant no harm.

"We brought Pinkie here because we're hoping she can make a bubble gum seal for the leak in the volcano," Melli told her. She turned around and saw Pinkie with her mouth gaping open.

"This is awful," Pinkie said softly. "Show me the crack."

Taking her hand, Melli and Pinkie left the butterscotch-covered ground and flew up to the side of the volcano to take a closer look at the leak.

 53

"Here it is," Melli said, pointing. "You can see how the butterscotch is pooling on the flat land."

Pinkie stared at the volcano for a minute. "Wow, that's a mighty big crack."

"Do you think you can make enough bubble gum for us, Pinkie?" Melli asked. She knew seeing the sticky situation firsthand had made her want to help.

"I am going to try my hardest," Pinkie told her. "I'll need more time and some extra Candy Fairy help."

"Take Berry and Raina with you," Melli said. "They will be excellent helpers. Dash, Cocoa, and I will stay here with Cara."

"That sounds like a perfect pink plan," Pinkie said. "Let's meet back here before Sun Dip."

Melli hugged Pinkie. "Thank you," she said.

"I'll see you later." Then she smiled at her cousin. "Good luck!"

While Berry, Raina, and Pinkie returned to Candy Castle, Cocoa, Dash, and Melli went to see how they could help Cara.

"Tula just dropped off more supplies," Cara said. She pointed to a few boxes lying on the ground.

"I can unpack and organize those things," Cocoa offered.

"I'll start cleaning these little birds over here, okay, Cara?" Melli asked.

"They've been waiting a long time," Cara said. "They'll be glad to be butterscotch-free."

For the next few hours the fairies worked hard washing caramella birds of every shape and size. When the birds were free of butterscotch,

they swooped through the air,  happy to fly once again.

"I've cleaned so many birds, but there are still more who are covered in this goo," Melli told her friends.

"It's a butterscotch disaster, all right," Dash sighed. Then she bent down to dip her finger in the thick butterscotch pool. "But I have to admit, this syrup is *really* delicious," she said, licking her finger.

"Leave it to Dash to still have an appetite even during a full-on Candy Kingdom emergency," Cocoa said. She crossed her arms across her chest.

For the first time since Melli had spotted the first butterscotch-coated bird, she laughed.

Dash's stomach was reliable—she was hungry all the time!

"I'm serious," Dash said, blushing.

Cocoa started to laugh. "I know you are," she said, smiling. "Believe me, I wish I could use all this good butterscotch. What a waste."

Melli's face lit up. "Hot caramel!" she screamed.

Dash and Cocoa looked at her. "What happened?" they said at the same time.

Fluttering her wings excitedly, Melli flew up in the air. "Nothing happened," she explained. "Except that you both gave me a *sugar-tastic* idea!" When she saw that her friends still looked confused, she said, "The butterscotch is delicious, and it is a shame that fairies can't use the syrup. This is an awful waste."

"Why is she saying what we already know?" Dash whispered to Cocoa.

"Because you're right!" Melli exclaimed. "We need to store and save the butterscotch. Let's get those big barrels from Candy Castle here and fill them with butterscotch."

"Sweeeeet!" Dash cheered.

"Maybe that would lower the level of the syrup pool here too," Cocoa said. "Look how high the butterscotch is now."

Dash held up her hand. "Wait a minty minute. *How* are we going to get the syrup into the barrels? And how are we going to get the barrels from the castle here to Caramel Hills?"

Melli sighed. "I didn't think of that. Any ideas?"

"Where's Raina with her Fairy Code Book when you need her?" Cocoa said with a sigh.

 59

Melli thought back to the last Butterscotch Festival. She remembered there were tubes set up from the volcano that led to the caramel barrels. "We need tubes," she said. "Something to pour the syrup in and move it from one place to another." She turned to Dash. "What would you make a tube out of?"

Dash thought for a moment. She snapped her fingers. "Toffee," she called out. "It's strong and slippery. I think toffee candy will be perfect."

Melli gave Dash a hug. "Sure as sugar, this is going to work! Dash, you get the toffee, and Cocoa and I will get the barrels."

"*So mint!*" Dash said. "I know just the toffee tree to visit for a good strong piece. It might take me a while to carve out a tube, but I'll try."

"Dash," Melli said, "I'm sure you'll do a

sugar-tastic job! We'll meet you back here before Sun Dip."

Feeling a burst of energy, Melli and Cocoa flew back to Candy Castle. Melli knew they'd find a large barrel there for them to take back to hold the butterscotch. Now all the syrup would not go to waste. And maybe, just maybe, they could stop the spill from spreading all over Sugar Valley.

7

Supersweet

At Candy Castle there were fairies flying busily around. With the kingdom in a state of emergency, everyone in Sugar Valley was helping out. So many fairies cared about Caramel Hills.

"There's Tula," Melli said. "Cocoa, let's ask her about finding some empty barrels. I'm sure she can help us."

The two fairies flew over to Tula, who was surrounded by a large group of fairies. She had a scroll and a long feather pen in her hands.

"Lemona, please take your crew of Sour Orchard Fairies to the animal rescue center set up in Caramel Hills," Tula said. "You'll find Cara the Caramel Fairy there, and she will advise you."

Melli's heart swelled with pride. She wanted to shout, "That's my little sister!" She watched as the group of Sour Orchard Fairies flew off. Berry was friends with Lemona. One time Berry had even gone to Sour Orchard, and Lemona had been very nice to her. Once again Melli was touched that so many fairies wanted to help.

"We're next," Cocoa said, pulling Melli closer to Tula.

Tula didn't even look up from her scroll. Melli wasn't sure if she should speak first. She looked over at Cocoa, who nodded toward Tula.

"Go ahead," Cocoa urged her friend. "Tell her your plan."

Melli cleared her throat. She suddenly felt as if her voice would not come out. She took a deep breath. "Tula," she said, "we have an idea about storing the overflow of butterscotch from the volcano."

Tula peered over her sugarcoated glasses at the two young fairies in front of her.

Cocoa squeezed Melli's hand, encouraging her to go on.

"You see, the extra butterscotch is causing so much trouble," Melli said quickly. "If we can get some of the syrup into barrels like we did at the

 65

Butterscotch Festival, we could stop the overflow and save the butterscotch syrup for later." Melli waited as Tula turned her gaze on her.

"Your name is Melli, right?" Tula said, staring at her.

"Yes," Melli said quietly. She stood perfectly still. She hoped that Tula thought she had a good idea.

"Melli," Tula said. She took off her glasses and looked into Melli's eyes. "Not one other fairy here has come up with such a good suggestion."

Melli looked down at her feet and fluttered her wings.

"Princess Lolli is not here," Tula went on. "She is at Butterscotch Volcano. But I think that is a supersweet idea. I like when a fairy is thinking! We'll have to get some of the palace guards to carry the large barrels over to Caramel Hills. Will you fly with them and direct the project?"

"Sure as sugar!" Melli replied. "I would be happy to show them where to go."

"Let me speak to the guards, and you can meet them out by the Royal Gardens," Tula said. "Give me about ten minutes."

"Thank you!" Melli said, bursting with pride.

Cocoa pulled Melli's hand. "While we're waiting, let's see how Pinkie is doing," she said.

Melli and Cocoa flew over to the bubble gum garden, just outside the Royal Gardens gate. In the middle of the garden Melli saw Berry, Raina, and Pinkie standing over a wide barrel.

"How is everything going?" Melli asked as she landed next to Pinkie. She looked into the bowl and saw a mound of pink gum.

Pinkie pulled the long paddle out of the barrel. Stretching her arm up high, she showed off the fresh batch of bubble gum. "Berry and Raina have helped me so much," she said. "With their encouragement and their sweet ways, I think we've made the largest wad of bubble gum ever!"

The pink sticky candy looked good enough to eat—and sticky enough to plug up a crack. "I think you're right!" Melli exclaimed. She clapped her hands together.

Cocoa filled them in on the plan with the barrels and Dash's project of building a tube for the butterscotch syrup.

"Good thinking," Raina said.

Melli blushed. "I remembered a chapter in the Fairy Code Book about the Butterscotch Festival," she said.

Raina's eyes sparkled. "Ah, you did!" she said. "Lickin' lollipops!"

"We need to make some more bubble gum," Pinkie told her cousin. "That volcano crack was very wide and deep. We should probably make another batch this size."

Melli agreed. "We still have a little more time before Sun Dip," she said. "Cocoa and I are going to fly back to Caramel Hills with the barrels. Will you meet us there?"

"Yes," Pinkie said. "Before Sun Dip for sure—just as we planned."

"You'll need some guards to fly this gum over to Caramel Hills," Melli told her friends. "There's no way you'll be able to pick up this barrel!"

Raina laughed. "We already spoke to Tula

about getting guards to help us," she said. "Don't worry. We'll see you later."

Melli and Cocoa and four palace guards flew back to the volcano with four large barrels. The barrels might not hold all the overflowing butterscotch, but it was a start. And that was the best she could hope for right now.

8

A Sticky Plan

Back at Caramel Hills there was a swarm of fairies flying near the volcano. Melli's heart started to pound.

"Maybe something awful has happened while we were at Candy Castle," she said to Cocoa. She tried to see the volcano, but there were too many fairies in the way. "I can't see a thing!" she cried. "Do you think the volcano erupted? Oh, that would be awful! Then there'd be even more butterscotch flowing over Caramel Hills."

Cocoa shook her head. "Just calm down," she said. "If Berry were here, she'd tell you not to dip your wings in syrup yet." Flapping her wings, Cocoa leaped higher in the air and squinted her eyes.

"Do you see anything?" Melli called up to her. She couldn't bear the thought of more syrup rushing over the hills.

"Nothing happened, I think!" Cocoa shouted. "Come up here. I see Princess Lolli." She pointed to the center of the crowd. "There are a bunch of castle guards surrounding her. She must be here to see the volcano firsthand."

Melli flew up next to Cocoa. It was easy to

spot Princess Lolli's strawberry-blond hair and her sugarcoated sparkly tiara. She was examining the crack and the damage done by the hot, sticky syrup.

"I want to tell her about our plan with the barrels," Melli said. "I'm sure she'll be pleased." She darted quickly in and out of the crowd to where Princess Lolli was talking to one of her advisers.

"Princess Lolli," Melli called. She waved and flew close to her.

"Hello, Melli," Princess Lolli said. "How is Pinkie coming along with the bubble gum? We will need a very big wad of gum to plug this crack."

"She's working on it," Melli informed her. "Berry and Raina are helping out." She took a deep breath. She was so anxious to tell Princess Lolli her idea about saving some of the overflowing butterscotch that she was having trouble breathing!

Princess Lolli put a hand on her back. "What is it, Melli?" she said kindly. "Is there something more?"

"Yes," Melli said. "Cocoa and I have another idea that might save the butterscotch and stop some of the overflow. We spoke to Tula about the plan. Would you like to hear it?"

Princess Lolli's eyes widened. "I'd love to hear some good news, or at least a good idea right about now," she said.

Melli explained the plan while Cocoa showed

the castle guards where to put the barrels.

"We thought if we could capture some of the butterscotch, the spill wouldn't get wider," Melli told the princess.

Princess Lolli's wings fluttered. "This is a fine idea," she said, "but how will we get the butterscotch into the barrels?"

Dash flew up behind the princess and Melli with a long, narrow toffee tube in her arms. "With this!" she cried. "We can stick it in the crack and seal the gum around the tube. Then all the butterscotch will flow through it and into the barrel."

Princess Lolli examined the tube. A smile spread across her face. "Sure as sugar, it's worth a try!" she declared.

"The bubble gum should be ready before Sun

Dip," Melli said. She looked up to the sky. It would be a little longer before the sun touched the tips of the Frosted Mountains.

"We'll have to be patient," Princess Lolli said, seeing disappointment in Melli's face. "I'm going to check in with the rescue center. Keep an eye out for Pinkie and the others. Send for me when they arrive so we can all be a part of Bubble Gum Rescue."

Melli watched Princess Lolli as she flew away from the volcano and back down to the animal rescue center. Normally, the princess had a lovely smile on her face. But today, Melli noticed, there was a deep crease in her forehead and she looked very troubled. She knew that seeing all the animals in danger broke the princess's heart.

"We need the bubble gum now," Melli said.

"Don't worry," Cocoa said. She was back from helping the guards with the barrels. "Pinkie will come. For now we should go help at the animal rescue center, don't you think?"

Melli followed Cocoa down to the base of the volcano and joined the other fairies. Working together made the task go faster, and time moved quickly.

After Melli finished washing her fifth caramella bird, she glanced up at the sky. The sun was nearing the tip of the Frosted Mountains.

Where is Pinkie? She has to get here! Melli thought.

Cocoa could see that her friend was worrying more and more. "Let's go back up to the volcano," Cocoa said to Melli. "They should be back soon."

Together, the two fairies hovered in the sky,

and just then Melli saw Berry, Raina, Dash, and Pinkie flying toward the volcano. Behind them were four palace guards holding the two large barrels of pink bubble gum.

"We've got bubble gum!" Berry announced as she drew closer. "Bubble Gum Rescue is ready to begin!"

"That is sweet news to hear on this dreadfully gooey day," Melli called. She flew up to Pinkie and gave her a hug. "I knew you could do this!" she cried.

"Pinkie whipped up the biggest and the stickiest bubble gum batch ever," Raina added.

"And I wouldn't have been able to do it without Berry and Raina's help," Pinkie told her cousin.

"Cocoa, go get Princess Lolli," Melli said. "Tell her we're ready to start the rescue!"

"I'll be back in a flash," Cocoa said, speeding down to the bottom of the volcano.

"Pinkie, all this bubble gum is fantastic!" Melli said. She peered into the barrel. "This just has to work!" she cried.

"I hope so," Pinkie said. She couldn't take her eyes off the large crack in the side of the mountain.

"Bubble Gum Rescue will work," Melli said. "You'll see."

She crossed her fingers and hoped that her prediction would come true.

CHAPTER
9

Pink and Positive

Melli and her friends hovered near the crack on the side of Butterscotch Volcano, waiting for Cocoa to return with Princess Lolli. *Oh, please hurry,* Melli thought as she kept watch for Cocoa and the fairy princess.

"What happens if there isn't enough bubble gum?" Pinkie asked as she hovered beside Melli.

"That crack is so deep. I'm not sure we've made enough to patch it up." Pinkie's pale pink wings were beating quickly, and her forehead was wrinkled with worry.

Melli was concerned too. She looked over at Berry and Raina, who were bobbing up and down in the wind. If only she could be as calm as her friends!

"Don't worry, Pinkie," Melli managed to say. "Whatever you made will help. Let's try to think positive."

Pinkie nodded. "I'll try," she said. "Pink and positive," she muttered over and over.

When Melli spotted Cocoa and Princess Lolli, she waved both her arms in the air and called out to them. "Over here! Oh, sweet sugar, they're finally here."

Cocoa waved back, and the two fairies flew toward them.

"Hello," Princess Lolli said, greeting the fairies. "Cocoa said that the bubble gum is ready. This is certainly sweet news."

"Yes," Pinkie said. "But we need help. The barrels of bubble gum are too heavy. We can't lift them."

"The guards are here to assist you," Princess Lolli said. She flew over and peered into one of the containers. "This is very fine work," she called. "Thank you." She smiled at Pinkie, Berry, and Raina.

"Let Bubble Gum Rescue begin!" Princess Lolli declared.

Then she turned to one of the castle guards. "Let's spread the gum around and see if we can seal the crack."

In a flash the guards moved the barrels closer to the volcano.

Dash took the long toffee tube she had cradled in her arms up to the crack. "I hope this works," she said. "We'll all need to hold the tube in place while the guards pour the bubble gum."

Melli saw Pinkie's confused expression, so she explained Dash's plan.

"We have some yummy ideas for all that butterscotch," Dash whispered to Pinkie.

Princess Lolli regarded the toffee tube. "This is *so mint*, Dash," she said with a smile.

Melli glanced over at Dash. She saw her minty friend blushing to the shade of red in a candy cane. "Thank you," she said.

"Oh, peppermint sticks!" Dash exclaimed. "It was the least I could do. I couldn't stand to see all that butterscotch wasted." She leaned in closer to Melli. "Promise me a special butterscotch candy later?"

Laughing, Melli hugged Dash. "Bubbling butterscotch, you've got yourself a deal!" she cried.

The Candy Castle guards poured the bubble gum from the barrels. With long, heavy paddles, they spread the sticky mixture into the crack.

Melli and her friends grabbed one end of the tube, holding it in the crack as the guards filled bubble gum in around it.

"All right," one of the guards called. "You can let go. The tube is secure."

The five fairies held their breath and flew up in the air.

"I don't know if I can look," said Cocoa.

"Yes, you can! Open your eyes, Cocoa. It's a sweet surprise!" said Melli.

No more butterscotch was leaking out of the volcano's side! Instead, a steady stream of the golden syrup was pouring out of the tube—and into a large barrel off to the side.

"Hot butterscotch!" Melli cheered.

"We did it!" Cocoa shouted.

A roar of applause rose up in Caramel Hills. All the fairies rejoiced and sang out. Bubble Gum Rescue was a huge success!

Melli rushed over to Pinkie. "Thank you," she said. "I knew you could do this."

Pinkie squeezed her cousin tight. "I never would have thought of this idea. Thank you for dreaming it up." She turned to face Berry and Raina. "And thank you, too!"

 88

"We were happy to lend some sugar," Raina said, grinning.

"Sweet strawberries," Berry said, coming up to Pinkie. "You did all the work, Pinkie. You should be extra-proud."

This was a time to celebrate, but Melli couldn't stop thinking of the caramella birds at the base of the volcano. There were still many suffering because of the butterscotch spill.

"What's wrong, Melli?" Cocoa asked. "You don't look happy. You should be! We just stopped the gushing butterscotch—and even managed to save the syrup."

Melli looked down at her feet. "I know," she said softly. She couldn't even speak about the awful thought that had popped into her head. "But . . ." She couldn't get the words out.

 89

Raina flew up next to her. "Are you worried about the caramella birds?" she asked. "Why don't we check in on the rescue center now?"

Melli hoped the animals in the center would be all right—especially if all the Candy Fairies continued to help. But that was not the only thing bothering her.

"Tell us," Cocoa said. "Please."

Melli bit her nails. "It's just . . ." She knew she had to say the words quickly, otherwise she wouldn't be able to tell her friends. Melli took a deep breath. She started to explain. "Now the crack is sealed and the gushing butterscotch syrup stopped." She paused and looked at the concerned faces surrounding her. "But what if this happens again?" Melli asked, her voice trembling. She watched her friends' expressions.

Each Candy Fairy had the same sad look. They were thinking the same sour thought.

None of them could have predicted what had happened in Caramel Hills. And they wouldn't be able to prevent the volcano from cracking or erupting.

Melli looked to each of her friends. But she knew that none of them had a magic answer for her.

CHAPTER
10

Bubbles of Happiness

Melli's question hung in the air. None of the fairies knew how to respond. Luckily, Princess Lolli was close enough to hear the question, and she immediately flew to the fairies.

"Melli, you asked a very good question," Princess Lolli told her. "There are many events we can be prepared for in Sugar Valley. We can try to prevent sour things from happening, but there is much we can't predict or prevent." She motioned for the fairies to move closer. When the fairies were huddled together, she continued. "Sadly, many events that happen are out of our control."

"Like a volcano leaking," Melli said.

"Or a river overflowing," Cocoa added.

"Even a rainstorm," Raina said softly.

"Yes, there are many things that happen naturally here in the valley," Princess Lolli said. "But working together can make life sweeter and safer. All the fairies in the kingdom should feel very proud for lending a helping hand."

Raina took the Fairy Code Book from her bag and showed the first page. "That's what the Fairy Code Book says too." She read, "'Nature can't always be predicted, so take care and be aware.'"

Princess Lolli nodded. "We all need to watch out for one another . . . and keep an eye out for leaking volcanoes!"

All of a sudden Cara came racing up to the group. "Please, come quick!" she cried.

"What's happened?" Melli asked. Cara looked upset, and Melli worried one of the caramella birds might be seriously injured.

"Please," Cara begged. "Come now!"

The fairies raced quickly to the animal rescue center. Melli could hardly breathe she was so nervous.

But once there Melli found quite a sight. Instead of finding a seriously wounded caramella, she saw a group of birds happy and clean.

"The caramella birds want to thank you all for your clever work," Cara said proudly. "I was bursting to tell you, but I promised that I would make this a surprise."

Melli hugged her little sister. "You've been pure as sugar," she said. "Thank you for helping so much with the rescue center."

"This is the sweetest part of the day," Cara said, hugging her sister. "I'm so glad that Caramel Hills is almost back to normal.

"With extra butterscotch!" Dash blurted out.

She looked around at the barrels of butterscotch that had already been filled. "It's like the Butterscotch Festival has come early this year."

"Dash, that is an excellent idea," Princess Lolli said, smiling. "Why not have a celebration now? All the fairies worked so hard to rescue the caramellas and save Caramel Hills. I think we should have a party!"

"A bubblicious party!" Pinkie exclaimed.

"I couldn't think of anything more fitting for this occasion," the princess proclaimed.

With a declaration from Princess Lolli, the fairies started to fly . . . and soon the rescue center had been turned into a place fit for a royal celebration.

Pinkie, Berry, and Raina were a *sugar-ific* team again and created delicious bubble gum bubbles.

"A rainbow of bubbles," Melli said when she saw the colorful decorations. "A sweet touch since the whole rescue mission was made possible by bubble gum!"

Cocoa and Melli joined several other Candy Fairies to whip up butterscotch candies.

"I'm so happy this butterscotch didn't go to waste," Cocoa said as she arranged the trays of freshly made candies.

Dash popped a candy into her mouth. "Mmm, you can say that again," she said, licking her lips.

Everyone in Sugar Valley was enjoying the festivities in Caramel Hills. "Nothing like a delicious turn of events," Melli whispered to Raina.

"How sweet it is," she agreed.

A caramella bird landed on Melli's shoulder and nuzzled her neck.

 98

"Hey, little sweets," Melli said, recognizing the yellow bird. "Weren't you covered in butterscotch the last time I saw you?" She rubbed the bird's neck and listened to the soft cooing. "I'm glad you are feeling better," she said. "Now let's try to keep you clean—and safe!"

The bird flew off into Caramel Hills. Melli smiled. She watched her friends enjoying Sun Dip in Caramel Hills. She felt relieved that once again her home was clean.

The quiet and still Butterscotch Volcano stood behind her. She eyed the bubble gum patch on the side. Princess Lolli was right: There was no way to predict another crack or sticky spill. But Melli knew her fairy friends would always be there for her—and the animals. Sure as sugar, Sugar Valley would stick—and work—together.

And that made Melli feel extra-thankful.

"Melli!" Cocoa called. "Everyone is loving our caramel chocolate rolls."

"It feels like ages since we made those," Melli said. "What a long day!"

Cocoa smiled. "Come on, you must try this *butterscotch* hot chocolate. It's double delicious!"

Melli flew over to where her friends and Cara were sitting. She took a cup and Cocoa poured her a serving of the hot, yummy drink. Then Melli raised her cup high in the air. "Here's a toast to bubble gum and to the best team of Candy Fairies!" she said.

The fairies cheered, and everyone enjoyed the sweet drink as the sun settled down behind the Frosted Mountains.

FIND OUT

WHAT HAPPENS IN

Double Dip

The sweet smell of peppermint made Dash's silver wings flutter. The small Mint Fairy was tending to her candies in Peppermint Grove. The weather was turning a little cooler, and there were many mint candies sprouting on the vines. This was perfect mint-chip weather! Dash picked a tiny mint pod from a stem in front of her. Carefully, she opened up the green pod, plucked the tiny mint chips out, and popped them into her mouth. "Mmm," she said. "Just right!"

"How are the new chips?" asked Minny. The young Mint Fairy flew over to Dash. "I've been waiting for those to ripen. How do they taste?"

"Perfect," Dash reported happily. She handed a pod to Minny. "Let me know what you think."

Minny put a handful of chips in her mouth and quickly agreed. "Yum, these are good," she said. "Dash, you are the master of mint!"

Dash blushed. She was excited about the mini mint chips. She thought they'd be perfect toppings for chocolates or even for ice cream. Just thinking about the yummy treats made her stomach rumble.

"Maybe we should take a break for lunch," Dash suggested. She rubbed her belly. "I'm starving."

Minny laughed. "Dash, you are always hungry!"

Dash couldn't argue. "I might be small, but I do have a huge appetite!" she said, laughing.

There wasn't a candy in Sugar Valley that Dash didn't love . . . although some she liked more than others!

The two Mint Fairies settled down under the shade of a few large peppermint leaves. Dash was thankful for the rest—and the delicious fruit nectar that she had brought for lunch.

"Oh, look, Dash!" Minny exclaimed. "There's a sugar fly note for you." She pointed to the fly circling over Dash's head.

Sugar flies brought messages to fairies throughout Sugar Valley. The flies could spread information—or gossip—to fairies far and wide. Dash quickly opened the note and then flew straight up in the air.

"Holy peppermint!" she cried. She zoomed around and then did a somersault.

"What did that note say?" Minny asked. She leaped up in excitement. "Must be extra-sweet news."

Dash flew back down to the ground. "I just got the best invitation," she told her friend. "You will not believe this. *I* can't believe this!" She shot up in the air again.

"What?" Minny begged. "Come down and tell me!"

"This is *so mint*!" Dash gushed. "Wait till all

my friends hear about this!" She scribbled off a note and handed it back to the sugar fly. "Please take this back to Meringue Island as fast as possible," Dash instructed. "My answer is YES!"

Minny's eyes grew wide. "Meringue Island?" she said. "Why, that's all the way in the Vanilla Sea!"

"Yes," Dash said. "And right near Mount Ice Cream."

Clapping her hands, Minny cheered. "I know—were you invited to race in Double Dip?" she shouted.

"Sure as sugar!" Dash said, flipping in the air again.

"Dash, that is minty cool!" Minny exclaimed. "I've only read about that race. And now you are going to be in it!"

"I can't believe it," Dash repeated, landing back down on the ground.

Minny sighed. "I've never been all the way to Meringue Island," she said wistfully. "I've heard that the Cone Harbor Festival weekend is supersweet. They have all these amazing flavors of ice cream and candy toppings for fairies to taste, and lots of carnival rides and parties." She blushed when Dash raised her eyebrows. "I read all about the festival in the *Daily Scoop*," she confessed.

Dash smiled. "I know. I've read those articles too! The festival seems totally mint," she said. "And I've heard the Double Dip course is one of the most challenging sled races. The race is the last day of the festival."

"Does that mean you'll have to race against

Menta and Peppa?" Minny asked. "They've been the champions for the past two years."

"So you know about those Mint Fairies?" Dash said, raising her eyebrows. "They make mint ice cream and live on Meringue Island. They definitely have an advantage because they've run the course so many times. But this year the race is going to be different."

"Why?" Minny asked, taking a sip of her drink.

"Because this year *I'm* in the race!" Dash boasted proudly. "I've never been to Mount Ice Cream. But now that I've been invited to go, I can't wait! It's not every day that a fairy gets invited to race in Double Dip!" Dash's mind started to flood with ideas. "I can't wait to start working on a new sled. I'll need a double sled for this race," she explained. "And I know just the partner to pick to ride with me."

"Who?" Minny asked. She leaned in closer to Dash.

"The perfect fairy for the job," she said. "She's fearless, and she knows chocolate inside and out."

"Oh, I've read there is that chocolate-coated part of the course," Minny said. She tapped her finger on her head. "I've heard that is the part where lots of fairies fall off their sleds."

"Exactly!" Dash exclaimed. "So with my secret chocolate partner, I'll have the winning edge."

"And a good friend to race with," Minny said, giggling. "I know you are talking about your friend Cocoa. She'll be fantastic."

Taking a bite of a mint, Dash nodded in

agreement. "I hope that she agrees. We'd make a *sugar-tastic* team."

Dash called over another sugar fly. "I wonder if Carobee the dragon would take my friends and me to Meringue Island. The journey would be so sweet on top of a dragon! I hope he will agree to fly us across the Vanilla Sea." She wrote her note and handed it to the sugar fly. "You'll find Carobee in the caves on Meringue Island," Dash told the fly. "Please hurry, and wait for his reply!"

Dash imagined the green-and-purple dragon getting the sugar fly note. She and her friends had met Carobee when they'd been searching for gooey goblins. While they had been looking for the mischievous creatures, they'd found Carobee. The fairies had become fast friends with the dragon after that adventure. Dash hoped that Carobee would be part of this adventure too!

The fly buzzed off toward Meringue Island. Dash leaned back and took a deep, slow breath in and out. "I just know this is going to be my year to win," she said. "To win Double Dip is a huge honor."

"And to beat Menta and Peppa would be a great accomplishment," Minny added.

"Hmm," Dash said, closing her eyes, thinking about the moment of glory. "Can't you see Cocoa and me in the winner's circle?" She sighed. "This is going to be *so mint*!" she exclaimed. "But first I have to ask Cocoa to be my partner!"

**Fly over
to meet the
Candy Fairies at**

CandyFairies.com

See what the Fairies left behind:

- A sweet eCard to send to your friends
- *Choc-o-rific* activities
- Delicious recipes

All you need to know about your favorite characters!

Looking for another great book?
Find it in the middle.

in
the
middle
BOOKS

Fun, fantastic books for kids
in the in-beTWEEN age.

IntheMiddleBooks.com

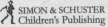